The Flying Horses of Watch Hill

WRITTEN and ILLUSTRATED by

LYNN ANDERSON

Flat Hammock Press
5 Church Street
Mystic, CT 06355
(860) 572-2722
www.flathammockpress.com

Printed in the United States of America

ISBN: 978-0-9795949-5-3

10 9 8 7 6 5 4 3 2 1

This book is dedicated to my father, Lawrence Anderson, who encouraged both his children to
work with their hearts and their hands, in woodcarving, sculpting and painting,
and to my brother, Gary Anderson, who researched, renovated and has maintained the Watch
Hill Flying Horse Carousel for the community of Watch Hill, Rhode Island, since 1993.

It is also dedicated to the Watch Hill Flying Horse Carousel, which, legend has it,
was abandoned in the town of Watch Hill by a traveling carnival in 1883,
and the caring community of Watch Hill that has built a roofed, open-sided carousel building
and faithfully cared for and preserved the beautiful little horses all these years.

It was almost a perfect summer afternoon. Sunlight sparkled off the ocean waves, and a warm breeze blew through the little carousel building at the end of Bay Street. The Flying Horse Carousel was the center of activity in the seaside town of Watch Hill. Children rode around and around on their favorite horses, listening to the organ music, waving to their parents, and—if they were very brave—leaning way out to try to catch the brass ring.

But the day was not quite perfect. Oh, no. It was the last day of summer. After today, there would be no more ice cream cones from the Ice Cream Shop, no more boxes of salty popcorn from the Popcorn Lady's popping machine. Worst of all, it was the last day the children would line up to buy their tickets and ride the carousel. Everyone in the little town knew that the summer season had come to an end. It was time to go home.

As the carousel began to slow down, the children riding the big horses in the row nearest the outside reached out for the last time to try to catch the brass ring, even though there would be no more free rides as prizes this season.

The carousel man stood gazing out to sea as the music faded and the horses came slowly to a stop. As he began to help the smaller children off the little horses, he sighed sadly. It was the last day he would see the children at the carousel, and he would miss them all winter until the carousel opened again next year. Some of them would be too tall next summer to ride the little horses.

The smallest children waited patiently for the carousel man to help them out of the leather saddles, while some of the bigger children reached up to their horse's wooden ears to remove the metal rings they had caught and stored there.

All the children had named their favorite horses, which they ran to every day when the gate opened. A little dappled horse named Benjamin was one of the smaller horses, who rode in the inner row and carried the younger children. The little girl riding Benjamin chose him every afternoon because she liked him best. Two years ago, when she first rode the carousel, she was so little that the carousel man had to help her climb into Benjamin's saddle. Now she could climb up all by herself.

When the music stopped, Ben's little rider put her arms around his neck. She stretched up toward his ear and whispered, "Good-bye Ben. I'm going to grow tall this winter, and next summer I'll be big enough to ride one of the outer horses and maybe even catch the brass ring!"

As the children slid down out of the saddles and said their good-byes to their favorite horses, the carousel man wandered slowly between the two rows of horses. He patted the mane of each horse and rubbed their ears, just as though the wooden horses were alive. He even spoke to them by name.

"So long, Ruby," he said. "Good-bye, Peg. I'll see you next summer. So long, old friend Dobbin. Bye-bye, little Ben."

He walked slowly toward the carousel gate, turning to look back and smile at his little friends one last time. Then he walked through the gate and was gone.

"Oh dear," thought Benjamin, as he watched the last of the children and the carousel man walking away down Bay Street. "I will miss them all so much. What will I do without the organ music and the carousel man and all my friends? What will I do next summer when the little girl rides one of the big horses? I'll be so lonesome. I'm just a little horse, but I wish I was a big fancy horse riding in the outer row."

Then the little wooden horse did a very extraordinary thing. He took a deep breath of sea air and sighed a long, sad sigh. If you had been watching as he sighed, you would have been surprised to see one large salty tear gather at the corner of his glass eye and roll down his wooden nose.

Ben turned to look at the other horses. His friends all looked as sad as he felt. Ruby sniffled quietly, and Peg whinnied softly. All the horses turned their eyes to look at Old Dobbin. He was the eldest and the wisest. They all waited for Dobbin to tell them what to do.

Old Dobbin snorted softly by way of introduction. He cleared his throat because he hadn't spoken all summer.

"Ahem," he said. "It's been a long and glorious summer season." All the horses murmured in agreement.

"We have stood proudly at attention each day waiting for the children to come buy their tickets and ride."

"Yes we have," they agreed, heads up a little higher.

"We have patiently ignored the little ones when they tweaked our ears and pulled our manes." Dobbin went on. "Once again, as we do each year, we have made the children very happy all summer long."

"Indeed!" "Absolutely!" "Hear! Hear!" the horses all chimed in.

"And now," Dobbin raised his voice just a little. "And now, the town is quiet, the carousel is closed, the children have gone, and our summer duties are over. No one is here to notice if we stay here or leave." Ears twitched and eyes were bright now. All the tears had dried as Dobbin finished his speech.

"Now it is time for us to leave the carousel for our winter home on Napatree Point!"

"Yes!" they all whinnied. "Here we go to run free on Napatree!"

At this, Ben gingerly stretched one leg and then another down to reach the floor. The other horses put their feet down too and began to wriggle out of their harnesses. They helped each other undo the clasps and buckles that held them to the turning framework underneath the roof. Soon they all stood stiffly on legs that had been raised in a galloping position all summer. They shifted their weight awkwardly from foot to foot. They stretched their necks, wiggled their ears, and made happy horse noises. It felt so good to be free and to walk on the ground again!

Dobbin looked up and down Bay Street and saw no one in any direction. With his muzzle, he nudged open the latch on the carousel gate and walked out into the late afternoon sun. Suki, Samantha, and some of the other younger horses couldn't wait to walk out the gate, so they bounded over the fence and landed on the sidewalk, teetering briefly on rubbery legs in front of the ticket booth. Auntie Peg walked proudly and sedately out the gate with Dobbin and the other older horses. They all wobbled down the sidewalk, giggling at their awkwardness. But by the time they turned the corner, crossed the parking lot, and felt the sand of the long peninsula called Napatree Point under their horseshoes, they were running and jumping around each other in glee.

"We're FREE!" they all whinnied. "WE'RE FREE!"

At first, the excitement of running in the sand was almost more than Ben could stand. All the little horses—Ruby, Samantha, Pokey, Suki, Duncan, and the rest—ran wildly on Napatree Point, just happy to be free and to run down the wide beach and through the waves. Ben felt the rough grains of sand and the sharp beach grass scratching the paint on his legs. He caught his reins on a beach rose bush and dragged the branch as he ran, but he didn't care about that—he just loved running faster and faster, till his hooves no longer touched the sand, and he almost flew across the thorny beach roses and spiky bayberry bushes.

When he finally stopped to rest, he stood still on the sandy beach and looked up and down for his friends. His cousin carousel horses were all out of sight. He thought again sadly of the little girl, who was so excited about riding one of the big horses next year.

"I wish I was a big horse," he said out loud.

Just at that moment, Auntie Peg came galloping around a dune. Peg was an outer-ring horse, which meant that she was larger and more colorful than the younger inner-ring horses, like Ben. She was a sleek palomino mare with a shiny, flowing, cream-colored mane and tail and a saddle blanket painted red and blue. Ben joined her to nibble ripe red rose hips off the beach rose bushes.

"I want to be a big, fancy horse like you and ride in front on the outer ring."

"Well, I'll tell you a secret," Auntie Peg replied. "Little horses are important, too, Benjamin. You'll find out why. Just wait." She smiled kindly and galloped off. Ben wasn't so sure about this mysterious advice, but when he caught sight of the other horses playing tag between the sand dunes he knew that he wanted to play, so he shook his long mane away from his eyes, stretched his neck up as long as he could to make himself feel taller, and trotted off to play with his cousins.

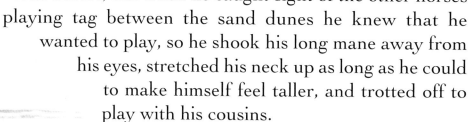

   As the days got colder and winter came to Napatree Point, the horses ran and played every day. They galloped through the waves at the edge of the shore. They ate bayberries and beach rose fruits, and they munched the beach grass that grew across the dunes and the salty seaweed that was tossed onto the beach by the waves. On cold nights, especially after dashing through the salt water, the horses gathered to sit in a circle. They huddled together to keep warm, and they listened as the older horses told stories about the famous carousel horses of long ago.

One cloudy winter afternoon on Napatree Point, Ruby came galloping past the dunes so fast that she hardly noticed when her long, shaggy mane got caught on a cedar branch. She slid to a stop in front of Ben with the branch knotted behind her ear.

"I saw the little red truck!" she announced breathlessly to everyone. "And I saw it first!" she added proudly.

Now they could all hear the distant cough-cough engine of the little red truck driven by their old friend, Mr. Gee.

"First one to the truck gets to ride up front!" whinnied Ruby.

They all broke into a canter along the sandy beach and then into a gallop down the dune path toward the oncoming truck.

Meanwhile, the little red truck was having a difficult time making its way along the beach. Mr. Gee was worried that his truck tires might get stuck fast in the deep sand before he ever saw the horses. His eyes scanned the tops of the dunes for the pointed ears and shaggy forelocks of his old friends, but he saw only the bleak, wind-blown dune tops with their dry brown grasses and the bare branches of bayberry rising against the gray sky.

Then he saw them. And what a sight they were, looking scruffy after a summer of wear and tear at the hands of loving children, followed by the winter's salty winds and blowing sand, which had scoured the paint off their noses, legs, and rumps. Their manes and tails were matted and full of thorny burrs. Bridles were dragging ends, and the beautiful saddles that Mr. Gee had made last year were torn and tattered. He looked at Ruby, whose left ear was broken, and Ben, whose right leg was wobbly.

"How will I ever repair them all in time for opening day at the carousel?" But his heart leapt as he saw them appearing, one by one, across the dunes. It felt so good to see his friends again.

"Mr. Gee! Mr. Gee!" The horses whinnied happily as they galloped toward him through the beach grass. Mr. Gee smiled as he recognized each scruffy little horse. He scratched their muzzles as their noses searched his pockets for the salty popcorn he always carried for them. As he patted each tousled mane, he laughed at the sorry state they were in. He counted noses to make sure that all the horses were there. First he checked the ten smaller horses, like Ben and Ruby, because they were younger and he worried about them the most. Then he moved to the ten larger horses, like Dobbin and Auntie Peg, because their old wood, fancy paint, and elaborate saddles had suffered terribly from the wear and tear of summer and the harsh winter.

"Hurry," said Mr. Gee, because the winter sun was beginning to set and a cold wind had begun to blow over Napatree Point. The little red truck's tires sank deeper into the sand, as each horse leapt up into the truck bed.

The red truck full of carousel horses chugged through the little town toward Mr. Gee's farm and the warm, cozy barn where they would live until summer came. Mr. Gee had cleared out the barn and started the wood stove early in the morning, so the barn was toasty. He patiently helped each horse up onto its special stand made from sawhorses and planks.

"Welcome back to the farm," he said, when everyone was settled. And then, because it had been a very long day, he banked the fire in the stove, closed the barn doors behind him, and walked up the hill to the farmhouse.

The barn was cozy-warm and smelled of new leather and paint. The horses were happy to be there, and they were soon very sleepy.

"Good night," said Dobbin to everyone.

"Good night," came muffled murmurs in reply.

The next morning, Mr. Gee came to the barn early. Out came the sandpaper, paint, and brushes. He arranged the tack hammer, tacks, new leather, and colorful fringe on his workbench. As he worked, his charges settled down to wait their turn. Scratches and bumps were healed with a special glue and sawdust prescription. Broken ears and legs were mended, splinted, and sanded. He took off worn and cracking paint with his special potion and rubbed the surface smooth. In the next few weeks, coats of shiny new white undercoat covered the sanded and primed wood, to be followed by colorful paint. Then noses, eyes, and dapples were redrawn with bright colors and dark black. Finally, a new coat of sparkling clear varnish covered everything and there were new blankets and saddles in bright new colors for each horse.

Many nights, Mr. Gee worked late to repair the old leather and make the new saddles and bridles in time for the carousel to open. He patiently combed the burrs and snarls out of all the manes and tails. Little by little, he transformed the once scruffy horses into twenty beautiful palominos, roans, grays, and dapples, wearing colorful saddles and bridles. While he worked, he listened to music on the radio, which reminded the horses of the carousel music they rode to all summer. Or, he would turn the radio off and hum a tune or talk to them as he painted the dapple designs, the hooves and horseshoes, and their beautiful black eyebrows.

This was a lot of work for Mr. Gee, and he was very tired, but the careful attention felt as good as a spring shower to the horses. They felt spiffy, handsome, bright, and full of energy for the busy summer ahead. When Mr. Gee went up to the farmhouse, they would gather in front of the barn windows to admire their reflections. When they saw him walking down the hill, they would scurry to climb back onto the sawhorses and stand proudly waiting for him. As he came through the door, he always stopped to look at all the horses and admire them. "You are the most beautiful carousel horses in the world," he would say. And the horses would blush red under their shiny new paint. They were all so proud.

One day, as Ben was admiring his reflection in the window, he saw lots of new green leaves on tree branches and pink azalea flowers in the woods behind the barn. "That means that spring has come and it is almost time to leave the barn to go back to the carousel in town," Dobbin told everyone. And sure enough, it wasn't long before Mr. Gee brought the little red truck down the hill to the barn and opened the two big barn doors. The excited horses were happy to take the ride back to the town beside the sea where the empty carousel building waited patiently. They missed the carousel with its flags flying and beautiful paintings all around the center. Soon they would be back in their places, the carousel music would start to play, and they would see the children lining up at the gate to ride the beautiful horses.

On the first day of the summer season, the carousel man walked between the horses, complimenting them on how well they looked with their new paint and saddles. Already the children were lining up to buy their tickets, and he greeted them as they ran through the gate to their favorite horses. Benjamin almost didn't recognize the little girl, who had grown taller just as she had hoped. Benjamin's heart sank at first, but then he saw that she was smiling and running toward him. She did remember him after all! And she was bringing someone else with her.

"Hello, Benjamin," she said, with a big smile. "This is my little brother. I've been telling him all about you, and he can't wait to ride the carousel. But Ben," she whispered as she put her head close to his, "my little brother has never been on the carousel before and he's a little scared. Could you be extra nice to him, please?"

Benjamin smiled inside. "I know about little children," he said to himself. "I know how to be extra nice so he won't be scared." As the carousel man bent down to lift the little girl's brother into Benjamin's saddle, he said, "This is the perfect horse for you, young man! This horse's name is Benjamin, and he is the best and gentlest carousel horse in the world. You don't need to be afraid, because Benjamin will take good care of you!"

The little boy put his arms around Benjamin's neck and whispered to his sister, "I like this little horse—he is just my size!"

The little girl ran over to Auntie Peg so the carousel man could help her climb up and find the reins. She was so proud to be tall enough to ride on a big horse that she couldn't say anything—she just smiled and hugged her beautiful new horse.

As the music began, the little boy held tight to Ben's neck and his mane, but as the horses slowly began to move forward, he sat up straighter and began to smile. Then he laughed as the horses moved around a little faster till they lifted up and he felt as if he was flying. From his spot on the inside ring, Ben could see the little girl. She was proudly riding Auntie Peg and leaning way, way out to reach for the brass ring and—she caught it!

That was when Benjamin knew that this would be the best carousel season ever!

EPILOGUE

"Mr. Gee" in the story is Gary Anderson, a wood carver, sculptor, and painter who was invited to renovate the Watch Hill Flying Horse Carousel in 1993. Gary researched the history of the carousel through newspaper articles, archival pictures, and other primary source information to find how the horses were originally carved, painted, and decorated. He removed many layers of old paint to find the colors first used, and he talked to carousel preservationists to learn how carousels were made, decorated, and maintained.

After repairing and repainting each horse, he cut leather and sewed saddles, bridles, reins and painted new blankets, and he bought horsehair and made new manes and tails. Finally, he painted the panels that form the center core of the carousel with paintings in the style of well-known painters of the late 1800s, when the carousel was new. Each year, after children ride the horses all summer, he carefully refurbishes the little wooden horses he knows so well and gets them ready for the next year. But he never starts to work on the horses until the middle of winter... so that they have plenty of time to gallop through the waves and play tag on the sands of Napatree Point.